Disney's Snow White and the Seven Dwarfs

Illustrated by the Disney Storybook Artists

Published by
Louis Weber, C.E.O.
Publications International, Ltd.
7373 North Cicero Avenue, Lincolnwood, Illinois 60712

Ground Floor, 59 Gloucester Place, London W1U 8JJ

Customer Service: 1-800-595-8484 or customer_service@pilbooks.com

www.pilbooks.com

p i kids is a registered trademark of Publications International, Ltd.

ISBN-13: 978-1-4127-6546-6
ISBN-10: 1-4127-6546-3

Once upon a time there lived a sweet princess named Snow White. She was very beautiful. She was so beautiful that her evil stepmother, the Queen, was very jealous. The Queen treated Snow White like a servant. She even forced Snow White to wear rags.

One day, Snow White made a wish at the wishing well. "I'm wishing," she sang, "for the one I love."

That very day, a handsome prince rode onto the castle grounds. He took one look at Snow White and instantly fell in love.

"Magic Mirror on the wall, who is the fairest one of all?" the Queen asked every day. And every day, the Queen's Magic Mirror answered, telling the Queen that she, indeed, was fairest.

Then one day, the mirror said something else. It told the Queen that Snow White was the fairest.

The Queen was furious and banished Snow White from the castle. Snow White was led deep into the forest by one of the Queen's servants.

A group of friendly animals saw that Snow White needed help. They led her right to a little cottage.

"It's adorable, just like a doll's house!" Snow White said with surprise.

"Oh, my!" Snow White said as she looked inside the messy little house. She guessed that untidy little children must live there.

Snow White got right to work. She dusted, scrubbed, and swept away the mess. She sang while she worked.

It didn't take Snow White long to tidy up the little cottage. She was tired when she finished cleaning. She went upstairs and found seven little beds.

"I'm a little sleepy," she said, and fell fast asleep.

"Heigh-ho! Heigh-ho! It's home from work we go!"
sang the Seven Dwarfs as they marched through the
forest after a long day's work. They were surprised when
they reached their cottage. It was not how they had left it.

Creeeak! The Seven Dwarfs opened the tiny door.
They searched every nook and cranny.

"Look, the floor! It's been swept," Doc said.

Suddenly, they heard a very strange sound. It came
from upstairs. They tiptoed up the steps to their bedroom.

Snow White was just waking up when she saw the Seven Dwarfs hiding behind their beds.

"Why, you're little men," she said, surprised. "How do you do? I'm Snow White!"

Snow White explained why she had to run away. The Dwarfs were scared because they knew the Queen was wicked, but they promised to help Snow White anyway.

Snow White made the Dwarfs a delicious dinner.
Then they sang songs and danced. Snow White told the
Dwarfs about the charming prince from a far-off land
who she hoped would someday find her again.

Meanwhile, the Queen thought Snow White was gone forever. The Queen was sure she would be the fairest one in all the land once again.

"Magic Mirror on the wall, who now is the fairest one of all?" the Queen asked.

"Over the seven jeweled hills," the mirror said, "in the cottage of the Seven Dwarfs, dwells Snow White, fairest one of all."

The Queen was furious! She disguised herself as an ugly old woman and made a special apple that would make Snow White sleep forever. The only thing that could wake her was Love's First Kiss.

"One taste of the poisoned apple," the Queen cackled, "and I'll be fairest in the land."

One day, after the Dwarfs had left for work, Snow White heard an old lady at the window.

"This is a magic wishing apple," the old lady said.

Snow White looked at the apple. She wished her handsome prince would carry her away to his castle.

Snow White took a bite and fell into a deep sleep.

The forest animals knew Snow White was in trouble.
They ran to get the Dwarfs, but it was too late. When the
Dwarfs came home they found Snow White.

They were heartbroken. They were sure their sweet
princess would sleep forever.

The Dwarfs made a beautiful gold-and-glass bed for
Snow White and put it in a field filled with flowers.

The Dwarfs kept watch over her. All the animals in the forest came to visit Snow White, too.

Meanwhile, the Prince, who had searched far and wide for Snow White, heard about the beautiful maiden who slept in a gold-and-glass bed. He came to get a glimpse of the sleeping princess.

The prince took one look at her and knew she was his true love.

The Prince gently kissed Snow White.
Her eyes slowly opened. Love's First
Kiss had broken the spell!

The Dwarfs and all the forest
animals celebrated as the Prince
carried Snow White off. The two
lived happily ever after.